W9-AAX-649
Noted 12-10-12
WITHDRAWN

BROWNSBURG PUBLIC LIBRARY
450 SOUTH JEFFERSON STREET
BROWNSBURG, INDIANA 46112

VISIT US AT
www.abdopublishing.com

Reinforced library bound edition published in 2010 by Spotlight, a division of the ABDO Group, 8000 West 78th Street, Edina, Minnesota 55439. Spotlight produces high-quality reinforced library bound editions for schools and libraries. Published by agreement with Warner Bros.—A Time Warner Company. All rights reserved. Used under authorization.

Printed in the United States of America, Melrose Park, Illinois.
092009
012010

Copyright © 2009 Hanna-Barbera.
SCOOBY-DOO and all related characters and elements are trademarks of and © Hanna-Barbera.
WB SHIELD: ™ & © Warner Bros. Entertainment Inc.
(s09)

Library of Congress Cataloging-in-Publication Data

Busch, Robbie.
Scooby-Doo in Barnstormin' banshee / writer, Robbie Busch ; penciller, Anthony Williams ; inker, Jeff Albrecht ; colorist, Paul Becton, letterer, Tom Orzechowski. -- Reinforced library bound ed.
p. cm. -- (Scooby-Doo graphic novels)
ISBN 978-1-59961-691-9
1. Graphic novels. I. Williams, Anthony, 1964- II. Scooby-Doo (Television program) III. Title. IV. Title: Barnstormin' banshee.
PZ7.7.B9Sc 2010
741.5'973--dc22

2009032896

All Spotlight books have reinforced library bindings and are manufactured in the United States of America.

Barnstormin'
BANSHEE
AAAA-OOOO
LIKE, GANGWAY, GANG! GET DOWN, COUSIN JAMISON!
YA CAN'T RUIN ME FARM NO MORE! YA FOUL BANSHEE!!!
ROBBIE BUSCH, WRITER ANTHONY WILLIAMS, PENCILLER
JEFF ALBRECHT, INKER TOM ORZECHOWSKI, LETTERER
PAUL BECTON, COLORIST DIGITAL CHAMELEON, SEPARATIONS
HARVEY RICHARDS, ASS'T EDITOR JOAN HILTY, EDITOR

HA HA HA HA HAAAAAA-OOOOOOO
VRRROOOOM!
UGH!
GOT YOU!
BLAST HIM! HE'LL NOT MAKE A FOOL OF *JAMISON P. WILLIKERS!*
WAA!
JAMIE, YOU FOOL! ARE YOU ALL RIGHT?!
I'M FINE, BETSY. AND NOW COUSIN SHAGGY'S FRIENDS KNOW WHY WE CALLED 'EM HERE!
MMM... METSY, MIS'S MMM-LISCIOUS!
MMM... RORE REASE!
SO THIS BANSHEE HAS SCARED OFF ALL OF YOUR HELP, JAMIE?
WORSE THAN THAT-- WE'RE SERIOUSLY CLOSE TO LOSIN' THE FARM. WE HAD A BUMPER CROP, BUT THE *BANSHEE* HAS SCARED OFF NEAR ALL OF OUR BUYERS. NOBODY WANTS *"WILLIKERS' GHOST CROPS"!*
WE'VE HELD ON LONG AS WE CAN, BUT IF WE DON'T MOVE SOME OF THAT PRODUCE SO… GO *BAD.*

AND YOU SAY THIS ALL STARTED VERY SUDDENLY?
CAN YOU THINK OF ANYBODY WHO MIGHT WANT TO CAUSE YOU TROUBLE?
I CAN...
...AND NOT ALL OF THEM ARE *LIVING*.
I THINK IT'S THE GHOST OF GREAT GRANDPA WILLIKERS! HE WAS ALWAYS ANGRY AT THE FAMILY FOR BEING STUCK IN THE SOIL. HE WANTED A FAMILY OF GREAT AIRMEN!
GULP! G-G-GREAT G-G-GRANDPA WILLIKERS?!
HE WAS A *CRAZY* OLD COOT! CAN YOU IMAGINE HOW HE WOULD BE FEELIN' NOW THAT HE'S *DEAD?!*
ZOINKS! I'D R-RATHER NOT IF YOU DON'T MIND!
I THINK I LOST MY APPETITE!
NOW, JAMIE-- DON'T GO FILLING THEIR HEADS FULL OF GHOSTS.
I THINK THERE'S A VERY *LIVE* PERSON WHO WANTS US OFF THE FARM!

WHO WOULD THAT BE, BETSY?
OUR CLOSEST NEIGHBOR, FARMER GORTLY.
HE'S BEEN FEUDING WITH US EVER SINCE WE CAME HERE!
GORTLY HAS WORKED THIS LAND FOR TWICE AS LONG AS WE HAVE, BUT WE'VE CONSISTENTLY GOTTEN BETTER CROPS THAN HIM!
RANK ROO!
HERE MA, I'VE GOT IT. YOU SIT AND REST.
WE OUGHT TO GO THROUGH THE HOUSEHOLD PAPERS IN THE CELLAR--
--AND SEE IF WE CAN DIG UP ANYTHING ON THAT MAN!
CRASH!
LORD! WHY ARE YOU SO JUMPY?
SORRY, MA! I'LL CLEAN IT UP!
WHAT'S SO FUNNY, BOYS?
SHE'S JUMPY 'CAUSE SHE'S GOT A DAA-A-ATE!
YER NOT GOIN' OUT WITH KIRK HAMMLEY?!
I'LL GO OUT WITH WHOEVER I WANT!

I TOLD YOU, YOU ARE NOT TO SEE THAT PUNK KID ANYMORE!
I LOVE HIM!
JENNY, GET BACK HERE! RIGHT THIS INSTANT!
WE ARE GOING TO BE MARRIED AND YOU CAN'T STOP US!!!
WE'LL LOSE HER, WE'LL LOSE THE FARM...WHAT ELSE CAN GO WRONG?
IT'S ALL RIGHT, JAMIE. COUSIN SHAGGY AND HIS FRIENDS WILL HELP US.
SURE, MR. WILLIKERS. WE'LL GET TO THE BOTTOM OF THIS.
AND DON'T WORRY ABOUT JENNY--SHE'S A GOOD KID. SHE'LL BE OKAY.
HERE, MRS. WILLIKERS, LET US HELP WITH THE CLEAN-UP.
JENNY REMINDS ME SO MUCH OF MYSELF AT HER AGE...
AND THAT'S WHAT WORRIES ME.

THE NEXT MORNING...
ZOINKS! THIS IS A BIG FARM!
GORTLY FARM
GOOD MORNING, KIDS. WON'T YOU JOIN ME FOR SOME LEMONADE?
IT'S NICE OF YOU TO SEE US ON SUCH SHORT NOTICE.
LIKE, NICE SPREAD!
WHAT MAY I HELP YOU WITH?
HAVE YOU HEARD THE RUMORS ABOUT WHAT IS GOING ON AT THE WILLIKERS FARM?
AH! THE BARNSTORMING BANSHEE, IS THAT IT? THAT'S A MYTH! I'VE WORKED THIS FARM FOR NEARLY 30 YEARS...
...AND I HAVE NEVER BEEN BOTHERED BY THIS SO-CALLED "BANSHEE"! NOW WHY DO YOU THINK THAT IS?
WELL, SIR-- WE WOULD ASK YOU THE SAME QUESTION!

STRANGE... THE MINUTE I ASKED HIM WHAT HE KNEW, HE WAS IN QUITE A HURRY TO SEE US GO!
I RIDN'T EVEN RET TO FINISH MY RECOND RECKFAST!
TRY, LIKE, THIRD BREAKFAST, SCOOB!
VERY STRANGE...
BUT NOT AS STRANGE AS WHAT'S BEHIND US!!!
LIKE, BANSHEE AT SIX O'CLOCK!
LIKE, STEP ON IT, FRED! BEFORE WE'RE BARNSTORMED WITHOUT THE BARN!
VROOOM!

EVERYBODY MAKE A RUN FOR THE HOUSE!
UH OH!
ROOK OUT, RELMA!
HA HA HA!!!
THUD
UNF!
THANK GOODNESS SHE ONLY GOT GRAZED. BUT WE SHOULD LET HER REST NOW.
LET'S GO OUT AND FIND THE BANSHEE!
UH...YEAH, YOU GUYS DO THAT! AND SCOOB AND I WILL STAY BEHIND TO LOOK AFTER HER!
PERFECT...
...FOR A LITTLE INVESTIGATING.

HMMM...
POOR GIRL. SHE'S IN OVER HER HEAD.
WHAT ARE YOU DOING WITH THAT?!
JENNY, I'M SORRY TO SNOOP. BUT I KNOW KIRK HAS BEEN PUTTING PRESSURE ON YOU. WHY DIDN'T YOU JUST ELOPE?
JOURNAL
I WANTED A PROPER WEDDING.
BUT NOW IT'S ALL RUINED!
LIKE, WHAT'S THE RUSH, JENNY?
SHE'LL BE OKAY, GUYS. BUT I NEED YOUR HELP.
JENNY KNOWS SOMETHING SHE ISN'T TELLING US.
HER JOURNAL-- AND HER BEHAVIOR LAST NIGHT-- MADE ME SUSPECT THE ANSWER'S DOWN HERE!
I KNEW IT! BEHIND JENNY'S THINGS...
WOW, LIKE, A HIDDEN TUNNEL!
JENNYS STUFF
RUNNEL!
AND AT THE OTHER END...
ZOINKS! THE BANSHEE'S SECRET LAIR!
VROOOM!
FLARES
RAND...REE RANSHEE!

WELL, IT'S NOT A SECRET ANYMORE!
FOOOOSH!
WHAT TH'--? THAT BARN'S BEEN ABANDONED FOR YEARS!
FLASH!
LOOK! IT'S THE BIPLANE!
ARGHH!
NO! THIS HAS TO STOP!
JENNY! HE'LL RUN YOU DOWN!
JENNY...
...I CAN'T HAVE YOU GET HURT OVER THIS!
IT'S OKAY...
...KIRK.
I'M SORRY, SIR. WE THOUGHT THIS WAS THE WAY FOR US TO BE TOGETHER...
... BUT IT ISN'T THE RIGHT WAY.
IT'S OKAY, HONEY! YOU SAW THAT IT WAS WRONG AND YOU MADE IT RIGHT. I TRUST YOU NOW MORE THAN I EVER DID.
LIKE, THEIR HARVEST WON'T SPOIL NOW! WE BETTER HELP THEM GET RID OF IT, HUH, SCOOB?
ROOBY ROOBY ROO!
HA HA HA HA HA HA HA
THE END

OVER A THOUSAND YEARS AGO, THE EMPEROR OF CHINA POSSESSED A MYSTERIOUS GLOWING GREEN STONE, FILLED WITH GREAT POWER, CALLED THE DRAGON'S EYE.
THE EMPEROR CUT THE STONE INTO SEVEN SMALLER, INTERLOCKING STONES, WHICH HE DISTRIBUTED AMONG HIS SONS. OVER TIME, THE STONES WERE SCATTERED AROUND THE WORLD.
NOW, SOME MYSTERIOUS VILLAIN IS STEALING THESE STONES. HE'S OUTWITTED THE MYSTERY INC. GANG IN PARIS, MOSCOW, ROME, AND DAMASCUS, BUT WILL HE BEAT THEM IN...
INDIA
SCOOBY-DOO IN THE DRAGON'S EYE PART 5
The KALI of the WILD!
JOHN ROZUM WRITER
JOE STATON PENCILLER
HORACIO OTTOLINI INKER
TOM ORZECHOWSKI LETTERER
PAUL BECTON COLORIST
DIGITAL CHAMELEON SEPARATIONS
HARVEY RICHARDS ASSISTANT EDITOR
JOAN HILTY EDITOR
CHARGE
WELCOM
NO LUCK, FREDDIE?
NO. OUR KHANSAMA* ASKED AROUND, BUT SAID THAT THE FOREST TEMPLE IS VERY SACRED TO THEM -- WHICH IS WHY THEY KEEP THE LOCATION A SECRET.
*COOK-CARETAKER
I'M AFRAID WE'RE NOT GOING TO FIND A GUIDE.
OH, NO! DID YOU TELL HER WHY WE WANTED TO GO TO THE TEMPLE?
THAT WE WANTED TO PREVENT THE THEFT OF EARRINGS FROM THE STATUE OF KALI?
YES. SHE SAID I SHOULDN'T WORRY. IF NO ONE WAS GOING TO GUIDE US TO THE TEMPLE, NO MATTER HOW HONORABLE OUR INTENTIONS...
...THEN NO ONE WAS GOING TO GUIDE ANY THIEVES TO IT!
INDIA
GUIDE

BROWNSBURG PUBLIC LIBRARY

BESIDES, SHE SAID EVEN IF THE THIEVES COULD FIND THE TEMPLE, THEY'D NEVER ESCAPE WITH THE EARRINGS!
WHY NOT?
BECAUSE THE TEMPLE IS SUPPOSED TO BE PROTECTED BY RAKSHASAS.
RAKSHASAS? YOU MEAN MONSTERS?
PHFSFSFSTTT!
WHAT'S THE MATTER, YOU TWO? DON'T TELL ME THE CURRY'S TOO HOT FOR YOU TO HANDLE?
NOT AS HOT AS A BUNCH OF MONSTERS!
LIKE, REMIND ME TO THANK EVERYONE IN TOWN FOR REFUSING TO TAKE US TO THE TEMPLE!
OH, SHAGGY! AFTER ALL THE CREEPY MONSTERS WE'VE RUN INTO TRYING TO SOLVE THIS MYSTERY, I CAN'T BELIEVE THAT YOU AND SCOOBY ARE STILL SUCH COWARDS!
LIKE, THE THREE OF YOU CAN SHOW YOUR BRAVERY WITH THE KOOKY WEIRD STUFF.
SCOOB AND I WILL PUT OUR COURAGE TO TACKLING INDIAN CUISINE LIKE ROGAN JOSH AND BIRIYANI!
RUMPTIOUS!

THIS CITY HAS A POPULATION OF OVER FIFTY THOUSAND PEOPLE-- IT'LL BE AWFULLY DIFFICULT TO FIND OUR THIEVES!
YOU'RE RIGHT, VELMA-- WE MIGHT AS WELL GO TO THE NEXT PLACE ON OUR LIST. AT LEAST WE'LL BE SURE TO BE AHEAD...
PSST. YOU ARE LOOKING FOR A GUIDE TO THE FOREST TEMPLE, ARE YOU NOT?
YES! DO YOU KNOW OF ONE?
I WILL TAKE YOU THERE MYSELF.
BUT YOU MUST TELL NO ONE THAT I DID THIS. IT WOULD BE VERY BAD FOR ME.
I WILL MEET YOU IN ONE HOUR. WALK ABOUT TEN METERS INTO THE FOREST AT THE END OF THIS STREET. BRING ONLY WHAT IS ESSENTIAL--
--AND THIRTY AMERICAN DOLLARS.
WELL, NOW THINGS ARE LOOKING UP!
YEAH-- UNLESS HE'S A ROBBER!
RETTER RAN A RONSTER!

I HOPE WE DON'T HAVE TO HIKE THE ENTIRE WAY. THIS FOREST IS TOO DENSE!
WELL, I DON'T THINK A JEEP OR TRUCK COULD PASS THROUGH THIS...
IT'S CLEARING OUT UP AHEAD!
NO VEHICLE CAN TRAVEL TO THE TEMPLE. IT IS VERY DIFFICULT TO REACH. THAT IS WHY WE WILL BE TRAVELING BY ELEPHANT MOST OF THE WAY!
I AM KRUTIN PATEL... AND THIS IS MY SON, SUNIL.
I HAVE HEARD THAT OTHER STRANGERS LEFT EARLY THIS MORNING WITH ANOTHER GUIDE, NAMED HADJI.
OH, NO-- THEY'VE BEATEN US AGAIN. OUR ONLY HOPE IS TO CATCH THEM AS THEY COME BACK FROM THE TEMPLE!
KLIK KLIK
I KNOW OF A ROUTE THAT SHOULD GET US TO THE TEMPLE AHEAD OF THEM. BUT EVEN IF IT DOESN'T, THEY WILL NOT GET PAST THE RAKSHASAS.
YOU BELIEVE THEY'RE REAL?
KLIK KLIK
HERE IN THE SATPURA RANGE, MANY STRANGE THINGS MAKE THEIR HOME. HUMANS WHO ENTER HERE MUST BE WARY AT ALL TIMES!

LIKE, I COULD GET USED TO THIS. NICE SCENERY. NO SOUNDS EXCEPT THE BIRDS AND BUGS. IT'S SO PEACEFUL!
KLIK
KLIK
EXCEPT FOR THE TIGERS AND PANTHERS WHICH HUNT HERE.
RYGERS? RANTHERS?
ZOINKS! LIKE, I THINK I SEE ONE NOW!
RELAX, IT IS JUST A BUFFALO.
PHEW
HEH-HEH I KNEW THAT...
ZOINKS, WHAT ABOUT THAT?
RHAT'S RO RUFFALO!
NO. NOT A TIGER, EITHER.
RAKSHASA.
OH, GREAT, A MONSTER! GIVE ME A TIGER INSTEAD ANY DAY!
ULP

NOW WHAT? THIS RIVER LOOKS TOO DEEP FOR THE ELEPHANTS TO WALK ACROSS!
ELEPHANTS ARE EXCELLENT SWIMMERS, BUT THEY DO IT UNDER-WATER WITH THEIR TRUNKS HELD UP LIKE SNORKELS. NOT THE BEST WAY FOR *US* TO TRAVEL.
BESIDES, WE ARE NOT *CROSSING* THE RIVER. WE WILL BE GOING *ALONG* THE RIVER. AND WE'LL BE DOING IT...
"...BY BOAT!"
WILL SUNIL BE OKAY BY HIMSELF BACK THERE?
OH, YES. NO JUNGLE ANIMAL WOULD DARE ATTACK TWO ELEPHANTS. HE'LL EVEN HAVE FRESH FISH WAITING FOR US ON OUR RETURN!
I JUST HOPE WE MAKE IT BACK FOR THE FRESH FISH.
LIKE, PLEASE TELL ME THAT THESE *RAKSHASAS* DON'T LIKE TO SWIM!
NO, THEY'RE NOT BIG ON WATER, BUT THEY'VE BEEN IN THE FOREST KEEPING PACE WITH OUR BOAT SINCE WE ENTERED THE RIVER.
GULP DID YOU SAY "THEY"?
YES, I COUNTED AT LEAST *THREE* OF THEM. THERE COULD BE MORE.
LIKE, ARE YOU SURE THIS IS A GOOD IDEA, FREDDIE?
I HOPE SO. BUT WE WON'T KNOW UNTIL WE REACH THE TEMPLE!

WE ARE VERY CLOSE TO THE TEMPLE NOW.
YES, BUT ARE WE ON TIME?
I ASSURE YOU, THE OTHER PARTY COULD NOT HAVE BEATEN US.
I STAND CORRECTED. THOSE ARE HADJI'S ELEPHANTS.
OH NO, WE'RE TOO LATE!
NOT THIS TIME!
SHAGGY, YOU AND SCOOBY GUARD THE ENTRANCE. IF ANYONE SLIPS PAST US, YOU MAKE SURE THEY DON'T LEAVE!
DAPHNE, VELMA, YOU COME WITH ME. KRUTIN, SHOW US THE WAY.
HEH-HEH, LIKE, MAYBE THESE GUYS HAVE SOME PEANUTS THEY CAN SHARE WITH US WHILE WE'RE WAITING.
WE LUCKED OUT THIS TIME, HUH, SCOOB? STAYING OUTSIDE, WHILE THE OTHERS GO INTO A CREEPY OLD TEMPLE!
UH, RAGGY?
GRRRRR!!
ZOINKS!

IT'S HADJI! SOMEONE'S KNOCKED HIM OUT AND TIED HIM UP!
OUR MYSTERY THIEF, I BET!
THE STATUE OF KALI IS AT THE END OF THIS CORRIDOR. HURRY-- I WILL STAY AND HELP HADJI.
SNARL!
GASP! WHAT WAS THAT?
COME ON-- WE'LL FIND OUT SOON ENOUGH!
STOP!
SNARRRRL!
OONFF!
CAREFUL, FREDDIE!
GRUNT! IT'S OKAY! UGH I THINK I GOT HIM!
HSSSS!

UH, WHAT ABOUT ALL THESE OTHERS, FREDDIE?
DON'T WORRY, VELMA. THEY AREN'T REAL!
SEE?
YOU FOOL! DO YOU REALIZE WHAT YOU'VE DONE?
BECAUSE OF YOUR INTERFERENCE, THE BLESSED EARRINGS OF KALI...
...HAVE BEEN STOLEN!
I SAW YOU REACHING FOR THEM, I -- UH -- THOUGHT YOU WERE GOING TO...
PROTECT THEM. WE ARE THE GUARDIANS OF THIS TEMPLE!
WHEN I HEARD YOU AND YOUR FRIENDS TALKING BACK IN TOWN, WE RACED HERE TO PLACE THE EARRINGS IN SAFEKEEPING!
WE CAN STRAIGHTEN THIS ALL OUT LATER.
THE FACT IS, WHOEVER DID TAKE THOSE EARRINGS COULDN'T HAVE GONE FAR.
BUT WE PASSED NO ONE, EXCEPT YOUR GUIDE AND THE INJURED MAN, WHEN WE ENTERED THE TEMPLE!

THEN THE THIEF COULD STILL BE HIDING SOME-WHERE INSIDE.
FAN OUT! SEARCH EVERY NOOK AND CRANNY!
DON'T WORRY, FREDDIE. IF THE THIEF IS INSIDE, THE RAKSHASAS WILL GET HIM. IF HE GOES OUTSIDE, SHAGGY AND SCOOBY ARE GUARDING THE EXIT.
JINKIES, WE'D BETTER HEAD OUTSIDE AND BLOCK THE EXIT!
NO FOOLING. C'MON!
THAT'S GREAT, SCOOB. LET ME TAKE A PICTURE!
CLIK
A FEW MORE TRICKS LIKE THAT, AND MAYBE WE'LL BE ABLE TO AMUSE THE OTHERS OUT OF BEING MAD AT US FOR LETTING THE RAKSHASAS PAST!
ROMEONE'S RUMMING!
PROBABLY THE OTHERS FLEEING IN FRIGHT!
CRITCH-CRITCH
NOW I'LL HAVE PROOF THAT WE'RE NOT THE ONLY COWARDS IN MYSTERY, INC.!

CLIK
GASP!
DAPHNE'S MYSTERY MAN!
DON'T LET HIM GET AWAAAAAY!
OOF! SORRY, SCOOB!
LIKE, GO GET HIM, GIRLS!
BRRR-RRNNNNNTTTT!
!!
SHROOP
SHROOP
SHROOP
YANK
OH, NO! HE'S GETTING AWAY!
CHUFF
CHUFF
WHIRRRR!
GRAB!

THAT'S THE MAN I SAW IN THE OTHER COUNTRIES!
AND--WHAT DO YOU KNOW--WE UNDERESTIMATED SHAGGY AND SCOOBY!
JINKIES! THAT FIEND IS POURING PEPPER INTO THE ELEPHANT'S TRUNK!
STAND BACK! SHE'S GOING TO...
KER-CHOO!!
NO! HE'S GETTING AWAY...
...AGAIN!
DON'T WORRY, FREDDIE. LIKE, WE'VE SCORED SOME POINTS IN THIS ROUND!
HOW?
WELL, THERE ARE STILL TWO MORE PIECES OF THE DRAGON'S EYE, AND...
...I TOOK A NICE CLEAR PICTURE OF HIM, SO WE'LL BE ABLE TO FIND OUT WHO HE IS!
GOOD WORK, SHAGGY.
MAYBE THINGS ARE LOOKING UP AFTER ALL!
TO BE CONTINUED...